Lily
and the
Yucky
Cookies

To my amazing son Weston, for listening to all my wild stories at night

—Sean Covey

For my sister, Shelley

—Stacy Curtis

SIMON & SCHUSTER BOOKS FOR YOUNG READERS
An imprint of Simon & Schuster Children's Publishing Division
1230 Avenue of the Americas, New York, New York 10020

For information about special discounts for bulk purchases, please contact Simon & Schuster Special Sales at 1-866-506-1949 or business@simonandschuster.com.
The Simon & Schuster Speakers Bureau can bring authors to your live event. For more information or to book an event, contact the Simon & Schuster Speakers Bureau at 1-866-248-3049 or visit our website at www.simonspeakers.com.
Book design by Laurent Linn
The text for this book is set in Montara Gothic.
The illustrations for this book are rendered in pencil and watercolor.
Manufactured in China
0617 SCP
4 6 8 10 9 7 5
Library of Congress Cataloging-in-Publication data:
Covey, Sean.
Lily and the yucky cookies / Sean Covey ; illustrated by Stacy Curtis. —First edition.
pages cm. —(The 7 habits of happy kids ; [5])
Summary: Lily Skunk bakes cookies for her friends without listening to her father's instructions.
ISBN 978-1-4424-7649-3 (hardcover)
[1. Listening—Fiction. 2. Baking—Fiction. 3. Skunks—Fiction.] I. Curtis, Stacy, illustrator. II. Title.
PZ7.C8343Lil 2013
[E]—dc23
2012051108
ISBN 978-1-4424-7650-9 (eBook)

SEAN COVEY

Illustrated by **Stacy Curtis**

SIMON & SCHUSTER BOOKS FOR YOUNG READERS

New York London Toronto Sydney New Delhi

THE EVERLASTING PEAKS
STEWART FALLS
LONE PEAK
GOOB'S CAVE
UNCLE BUD'S PARK
JUMPER'S HOLE
POKEY'S PLACE
THE MEADOW
CHERRY CREEK
LILY'S BURROW
TAGALONG ALLIE'S BURROW
MS. HOOT'S GARDEN

"Is it going to rain all day, Dad?" said Lily Skunk. "My friends were going to Fish-Eye Lake today. Now there's nothing to do."

"We can bake cookies," Lily's dad said. "It's a perfect rainy day treat."

"Yum," said Lily's little brother, Stink.

"I've seen Mom do it a hundred times. I know exactly what to do," Lily said.

"Well," her dad said, "let's check the recipe just to be sure."

"First you have to mix two cups of flour, a half cup of sugar, and a pinch of . . . are you listening, Lily?" asked Dad.

"Daaaad," said Lily. "I don't need a recipe. I know what I'm doing."

"Be careful, Lily. You're moving awfully fast," her dad said.

"It's all right, Dad. They'll be perfect." Lily finished mixing and her dad helped her put the cookies in the oven.

"Look, Lily, the sun is coming out!" Stink exclaimed. "You can go to Fish-Eye Lake now. Can I come?"

"No, you're too little. You stay home," Lily said.

Stink nibbled a cookie and said, "But, Lily, these cookies are . . ."

Lily didn't listen as she rushed off to Fish-Eye Lake.

"Hi, everyone! I brought cookies! I baked them myself.

I hope you like them."

"Oh, Lily, those look delectable!" said Sophie.

"Puh," said Jumper. "They taste like salt."

"I think I'm gonna throw up," said Pokey.

"Wiwee, da cookies are kind of gwoss," said Tagalong Allie.

Lily felt awful. She didn't know what went wrong. So she went home.

"Dad, nobody liked my cookies and Allie said they were gross and Pokey almost threw up and so I dumped them all in the garbage," said Lily.

"It's okay, Lily," said her dad. "You just need to listen next time. You don't have to follow the recipe exactly, but you want to make sure you

understand every step before you get started."

"Can we bake cookies again? I promise, promise, promise that I'll listen this time."

FLOUR
SUGAR

After dinner Lily and her dad went back to the kitchen to make more cookies. Lily listened as her dad read the whole recipe. Stink tried to help too, but he kept eating all the chocolate chips.

The next day Lily brought a new batch of cookies to her friends.

"These are much better," said Lily.

But no one wanted to try them.

“I’m not going to go first,” said Jumper.

Finally Allie said, “I’ll twy one.”

Everyone watched as Allie slowly put one in her mouth.

"Yup, yup, yup. These are the best cookies eveh, Wiwee!"

They all started grabbing and eating the cookies. Pretty soon they were all gone.

"Those cookies are so yummy for my tummy," said Goob.

"What's in them?" asked Pokey.

"Well . . ." Lily said, "the secret ingredient is listening."

PARENTS' CORNER

HABIT 5 —Seek First to Understand, Then to Be Understood: *Listen Before You Talk*

AS LILY HAD TO LEARN THE HARD WAY, SEEKING FIRST TO UNDERSTAND, OR LISTENING, is the secret ingredient of life. In general, there is way too much talking and way too little listening going on. Like Lily, we have a tendency to think we know it all, to rush in, to fix things up with good advice. We too often fail to read directions, to diagnose, to truly understand another person's point of view.

Seeking first to understand is a correct principle in all areas of life. A good writer will understand his audience before writing a paper. A good doctor will diagnose before she prescribes. A careful mother will understand her child before evaluating or judging. An effective teacher will assess the needs of his class before teaching.

In this story, Lily thought she knew it all and didn't take the time to listen. As a result, her cookies were yucky. When she took the time to listen and follow a recipe, the cookies were "yummy for my tummy," as Goob put it. And that's how it is in life, too. Listening takes time. Trying to understand where your spouse or colleague or child is coming from takes time. But it also produces a great batch of cookies. And it doesn't take anywhere near as much time as it takes to back up and correct misunderstandings when you're already miles down the road, to redo, to live with unexpressed and unsolved problems, to deal with the results of not giving people what they want most, which is simply to be understood.

Let us always remember that we have two ears and one mouth and we should use them accordingly.

Up for Discussion

1. What did Lily do wrong while making cookies?
2. Why didn't Lily pay attention to her father?
3. What happened when she gave the 7 Oaks gang the cookies at Fish-Eye Lake?
4. The next time Lily baked cookies, what did she do differently? What did her friends think about the new batch of cookies?
5. Why is it important to listen?

Baby Steps

1. Ask others about what you can do on a rainy day. Listen carefully and make a list.
2. Have a friend or sibling tell you a story. Listen closely and tell that story to someone else.
3. Talk with your mother and father about how you can be a better listener.
4. Go thirty minutes without saying anything, only listening.
5. Bake cookies with your mother and father and follow the instructions closely. Be sure when you make your cookies that you add your own secret ingredient.

THE EVERLASTING PEAKS
THE SAND DUNES
FAR NORTH WOODS
CHERRY CREEK
BEAVER'S DAM
GOAT ISLAND
LOLLIGAG HILLS
THE MISTY FOREST